cat's pajamas

THACHER HURD

TAYLOR TRADE PUBLISHING
Lanham • Boulder • New York • London

Cat's pajamas
Doodley-doo

Kitties on the prowl
Two by two

**Bopping down dark streets
Looking for CHOW!**

Then they play a cool song

BOOM BAM BOOM!

Cats on the kittyhorn
Cats on the drums

Big moon HOWL!

Hot night YOWL!

Kitty kitty kitty cats
GRRRRROWWWWL!

Put away the kittyhorn
Put down the drums
Off to Pajama Land
Rum tum tum

SWEET DREAMS

PAJAMA CATS

Yum yum yum